MW01115420

This book belongs to

Jacob and Sam Walters

Friends Of A Feather

One of Life's Little Fables

Friends Of A Feather

One of Life's Little Fables

by Bill Cosby

illustrated by Erika Cosby

HarperEntertainment

An Imprint of HarperCollins*Publishers*

FRIENDS OF A FEATHER: ONE OF LIFE'S LITTLE FABLES. Copyright © 2003 by William H. Cosby Jr. All rights reserved. Printed in the United States of America. No part of this book may be used or reproduced in any manner whatsoever without written permission except in the case of brief quotations embodied in critical articles and reviews. For information address HarperCollins Publishers Inc., 10 East 53rd Street, New York, NY 10022.

HarperCollins books may be purchased for educational, business, sales or promotional use. For information please write: Special Markets Department, HarperCollins Publishers Inc., 10 East 53rd Street, New York, NY 10022.

FIRST EDITION

Written by Bill Cosby
Illustrations by Erika Cosby
Illustration direction by Victor Cagno
Designed by Susan Sanguily and Jo Obarowski
Special thanks to Mel Berger, David Brokaw, Hope Innelli, and Liz Perle

Printed on acid-free paper

Library of Congress Cataloging-in-Publication Data has been applied for.

ISBN: 0-06-009147-9

03 04 05 06 07 PHX 10 9 8 7 6 5 4 3 2 1

This book is dedicated to all parents, children, and elders
who join to strengthen youngsters

Special Acknowledgments

I acknowledge the birds flying and diving over and around
the rock just off the Island of Guana, but not the iguana
that ate my blueberry muffins in the mornings.

— B.C.

They call me Slipper. The real name is Blank, but Slipper will do just fine.

I used to rule the skies out here on the beach. The beach has no name, so we just call it the Beach by the Rock.

The Rock stands all alone in the blue-green water by the cove, where the best and yummiest fish play.

This is not my story, but I can tell you why I'm the bird to tell it. You see, I was the bird. I mean THE BIRD. No one could touch me when it came to swoops, whirls, flips, and scores. Everyone who was anyone knew me.

Back then all us birds would swoop down around the rock, trying out one new trick after another but always respecting it because it was the Rock.

We flew for each other mostly. And though we were all something special, the others looked to me because I could fly high enough to meet the clouds eye to eye and I could also disappear just by making my blue wings blend into the sky. It was like I was invisible. And I would always return with tales about the cool things I saw hidden from most others' sight.

But all of that was before they came. The PEOPLE. People who lived near rocks of their own all over the world. People with children, blankets, coolers, and cameras.

Pretty soon these people covered every grain of sand on the dunes. There were so many of them that the birds almost decided to call the rock "the Rock by the People." But we didn't.

Anyway, all these folks came to see this one bird. Not me, mind you, but a bird named Feathers.

Feathers has a wingspan as large as a full-grown eagle's. And when he flutters those flappers of his, they sparkle brighter than a peacock's tail. All these colors glitter in patches and swirls.

Sometimes it's as if rainbow streams of light dance behind him like brightly colored ribbons tied to a balloon on a windy day.

It's hard NOT to love Feathers. He's so beautiful.

I suppose that next to him, I'm just an old tweeter with a disappearing act and stink plants growing under my wingpits.

It's true—every time I sweat, I sprout these nasty-smelling geraniums!

But not Feathers. When he sweats, he glistens. He spreads his wings and all you see is a medallion of red and white feathers shimmering across his breast.

People would go crazy when they saw that. "That bird must be magic," they'd whisper, and some would even make a wish as he streaked by.

Day by day the noise from the crowds rose. Where it was once just one person clapping, it became ten, and then ten more. The sound of people applauding grew hand by hand.

All Feathers had to do was swoop down from on high and the people would go, "Ooh." When he glided inland like a 747 approaching a runway, people would go, "Ahh."

Then there was always that moment, about 100 feet above the water, when he'd pull in those funky-colored wings of his faster than the snap of your fingers. You could hear them slap against his body. You'd think the crackle they made was as dramatic as THUNDER—the crowd loved that sound so much.

Feathers did have this one cool trick, which he just happened to learn from me. He could make himself look like a dart spiraling in the wrong direction.

The crowd would hang in silence on his every twist and turn. Then there'd be booming applause as he splashed down.

Within seconds, he'd poke his head up through the water with tons of fish in that aerodynamically sleek beak of his! The fish were always turned heads to the left, tails to the right!

If Feathers picked 'em up the other way around, then he'd just toss 'em right back in and still get an ovation.

Now the one young bird with a shot at pleasing the crowds more than Feathers was his best friend—a dude named Hog. He's called that because he kind of looks like a hedgehog. He has a stout body covered with prickly feathers. Only two colors, brown and gray, march in neat little rows across his short wings. But his shoulders are real strong and he has this bucket-shaped beak that not only parts waves, it opens sideways on impact.

As soon as Hog hits the water, he cracks a smile and swallows up half the ocean in one gulp. Look out, fish and shrimp! Too bad you can't yell "Help," kelp!

I tell you, Hog earns his nickname in every way. He even eats stones! And he burps water out through these holes in his stubby neck.

That Hog is really something else. He is the most daring of us all. And he can do a mean swan dive, too!

But the people on the beach never seemed to notice, no matter how many tough tricks he did. He always surfaced expecting to hear applause, but there would be silence instead.

I remember Feathers telling Hog, "Lately, you're always doing that swoop and snap thing. And you're getting closer and closer to that rock. Try one of those tricks again and you're gonna get flattened."

It's not like his feathers were ruffled or anything. Feathers wasn't mad at Hog for showing off. He just knew when enough was enough.

"Do you want to do a face plant into that rock the way Slipper did that time?" Feathers asked Hog, referring to one of my less wonderful moments.

"You remember. Slipper had to be the bird, flying higher and faster than the rest of us. But when the wind came, he got swept up and landed way too close to the Rock. I really don't like you guys challenging the Rock that way. What'd that rock ever do to bother you? So *please*, no more dangerous stuff," he pleaded. "Okay?"

After that, Hog stuck closer to Feathers.

Of course Feathers still did crowd-pleasing tricks. One time he spied a school of fish from way, way, up high, so he plunged right in.

CRACK went the water. For a moment all was silent.

Then CLAP, CLAP, CLAP went the people. Feathers surfaced with more good eats than ever—fish heads to the left, fish tails to the right! "OOOH," wrote the press. "AHHH," said the radio folks. "WHOA," cried the TV anchorman.

But Feathers wasn't nearly as impressed with himself this time. He shook his head in disgust and tossed the fish back into the sea.

"MY," said the journalist. "GOODNESS," said the boom man. "AMAZING," said the camerawoman. "WHAT DO YOU MAKE OF THAT?"

Hog hovered above. He heard the OOOHs, the AHHHs, and the WHOAs. He sure wanted the press to write about him that way. So he sped further up into the sky. Then, stopping in midflight, he leaned back, crossed his tiny legs, and tucked in his feet. Hog was ready to dive. He was going to do a double back flip pike!

It was all going so well till he saw the water below and froze.

WHAM! Hog hit the Rock by the Beach.

The crowd all laughed and clapped and cheered. They thought it was a comedy routine. But there was nothing funny about it.

Hog was in great pain. By the time Feathers swam over, he had tried to get up, but he couldn't. The wing he'd landed on just wouldn't flap anymore. Hog groaned and moaned.

"Where does it hurt?" Feathers asked.

"All over," bellowed Hog.

"Can you move it this way?" Feathers tried to lift Hog's wounded wing.

"OUCH!" Hog let out a Hog bird yell. "DON'T TOUCH IT! It hurts everywhere, from my wing tips to my toes."

Feathers didn't know what to do.

By now, Hog's injured wing was dragging on the water, and the clouds threatened rain. Each time the waves rolled in, Hog howled this terrible Hog-in-pain howl.

I know! Feathers thought. He dove under the water, centered his body beneath Hog's, opened his wings wide, and raised his friend up.

"Hang on!" he cried. Then they flew off together.

When the two birds landed safely on firm ground, Feathers scolded, "Didn't I tell you not to mess with that rock?" He checked Hog's wing more closely now.

"Lucky for you nothing's sticking out. Looks like all I have to do is snap this wing back in place." Hog closed his eyes, counted to three as fast as he could, then screamed, "AHHH."

"I didn't even touch anything yet!" said Feathers.

"Yeah, but you were about to and it was going to hurt," whimpered Hog.

"Okay, then, if you know so much," Feathers snapped, "how come you're the one with the broken wing?"

"You know what hurts even more right now?" Hog asked. "My pride. All those people watched me wipe out back there."

"Right now, that's the least of your problems," said Feathers. "Let's get you up on your feet so you can walk around a little."

"Okay, but my legs are so short, I hope my wings don't drag."

Suddenly, Feathers grew serious. "Hog, I want to ask you something. You're the best flier in the flock. You always try new tricks and you like taking risks."

"What's your question?" Hog interrupted.

"Why is that?" Feathers finally asked.

Hog thought for a moment. "I just like to," he said. "It feels good."

"Yes, I know, but I think you also do it because people never clap or make noises for you like they do for me. They never write about you or OOH and AHH when you do things I'd be too afraid to do. Why do you suppose that is?"

Hog didn't have an answer.

"Like that trick you did today was hard—really hard. That head-to-tail, head-to-tail, all-tucked-up, double-backward-pike thing you did. That was crazy! And they didn't even clap. They just laughed. I felt really sorry that you hurt yourself for those people."

Hog didn't know what Feathers meant. "I didn't hurt myself for those people," he said. "Maybe I hurt myself for myself."

"That's not true," said Feathers. "As long as we've been flying together, you never did anything that made me worry about you. Sure, you did silly things, but never something that could end up really hurting you."

"I didn't know you worried about me so much," said Hog.

"We worry about each other. You know that," Feathers said softly. "Those people on the beach are probably very nice, but what they think isn't important to me. So don't call out, 'Hey, Feathers, look at me do this or look at me do that' when they're around. When we fly alone you NEVER do that. All I am saying, Hog, is that you're my friend and I don't ever want you to hurt yourself again."

"I get it," said Hog. "All that's really important is us."

"That's right," said Feathers. "When we fly, we fly with each other. When we laugh, we laugh with each other. Those people don't know how to fly. They don't know our laugh. And they don't eat fish whole."

Hog smiled. He knew Feathers was right.

"Now look at that over there!" said Feathers.

"Where?" Hog turned his head, but he couldn't see a thing.

POP!

While Hog looked the other way, Feathers snapped his wing right back into place.

"AHHH," Hog whined. "That's not nice. You tricked me."

"I had to do it, Hog. You'd do the same for me if I broke my wing... and you'd enjoy it, too!"

"But what if my wing had fallen off?" Hog cried.

"Your wing wasn't in danger of falling off!"

"Yeah, you're just good-looking. You think that flexing those power wings of yours makes you special. Don't ever do that to me again. Promise?"

"Okay, I promise," said Feathers. "But you have to promise me something, too. When we eat, it's because we're hungry, when we fly, it's because it's fun. And you've got to forget about trying to get too close to the Rock and getting people to make noise for you. Okay? Do you want me to be scared again?"

"No," said Hog, rubbing his sore shoulder.

"Do you want your wing to pop out again?"

"No!"

"Are we good friends?"

"Yes," said Hog.

"Forever?"

"Forever."

This story could end here. It is a nice ending, after all. But since it's not polite to interrupt an old bird like me, and since I still sometimes see things others don't, I will tell you that the two friends took off from the cove and headed back toward the Beach by the Rock and the press and the people and the noise.

Hog sailed high into the sky above the Rock while Feathers huffed and puffed just trying to catch up.

"Remember what I said?" Feathers called after him. "No tricks."

"Okay," said Hog.

"I'm gonna be watching you," warned Feathers. "There are people down there. What are you gonna do?"

But before Hog could answer, he began to tumble. "MY WING, MY WING," he screamed.

"Oh no, not again! Hang on, I'm coming," Feathers cried. "Here, you can land on me!"

As Feathers braced for the thump that would be Hog landing on his back, all he felt was a swoosh of air passing.

Feathers looked up. No Hog.

He looked around. Still no Hog. Now he was panicked!

"Yoo hoo!" came a voice from below. There was Hog, floating on thin air. "Bet you thought I did that for the people," he teased. "But that's not true. I did it because you talk too much!"

Then Hog sped out of range, laughing as loud as I ever did hear Hog laugh.

Feathers was a little peeved, but he was also very relieved.

"Hey, you, HOG," he shouted back. "Better watch out. I'm gonna get you!"

The two birds chased each other, giggling, while the people on the beach applauded and took pictures. As the friends circled higher and higher, the OOHs and the AHHs got fainter and fainter until they could hear them no more.

World-renowned comedian, actor, and producer Bill Cosby is also a bestselling author. His celebrated works for adults include *Fatherhood, Love & Marriage, Time Flies,* and *Cosbyology,* while his *Little Bill* series books are runaway hits with children. He has appeared on such landmark television shows as *Fat Albert* and *The Cosby Show.* Bill Cosby earned a doctoral degree in education in 1977 and received the Presidential Medal of Freedom in 2002.

Erika Cosby is an accomplished painter whose work has appeared in galleries in San Francisco, California, and New York City. She received her BFA from the School of Visual Arts and her MFA from the University of California–Berkeley.